Rose Impey

Scare Yourself to Sleep

Illustrated by Moira Kemp

Mathew Price Limited

When my cousin comes to stay
we sleep in a tent
at the bottom
of the garden.
We don't let my brother in.
He'd spoil everything.

We love it
just the two of us
lying there
side by side
talking.

We tell each other jokes
very quietly
because we don't want anyone
to know we're there.

We know Simon is there
outside the tent
trying to listen
so we whisper.
We don't want him
spoiling everything.

Soon it starts to get dark.
The shadows rise
and outside it grows
quiet and still.
Then me and my cousin
always play the same game.
We call it
'Scare yourself to sleep.'

First I whisper to her,
'Are you scared?'
'No,' she says, 'are you?'
'No,' I say, 'but I bet
I could scare you.'
'Go on then,' she says.
'Right,' I say
and I tell her all about
The Dustbin Demons.

They are the gangs
of evil little goblins
who live
under the rubbish
in the bottom
of dustbins.

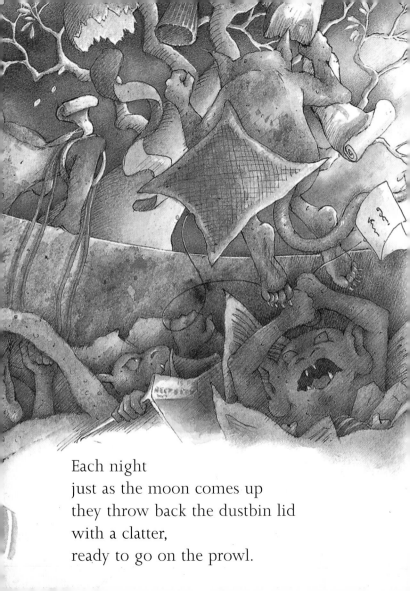

Each night
just as the moon comes up
they throw back the dustbin lid
with a clatter,
ready to go on the prowl.

They fling
all the rotten food
up in the air
then out they crawl,
climbing over one another
in their hurry to be off.
They swarm around the garden
until they find
some helpless creature
foolish enough
to be out alone.

Then they carry it off,
struggling and squealing,
back to their smelly den
never to be seen again.

My cousin is very quiet.
She wriggles down
into her sleeping bag.
I smile to myself.
That scared her.

Suddenly there is a
CRASH!
It sounds like a dustbin lid
banging and clattering
on the garden path.
Our hearts are thumping.

Then we hear, 'Gottya. Heeheehee.'

'Oh, Simon, go away.
You are stupid,' we say.
'You didn't scare us.'
But we move our sleeping bags
a little closer together
just in case.

Next she tells me about
The Flying Cat.
It creeps along
on its soft padded paws,
pretending to be
any ordinary cat.
But at the stroke of
midnight it sprouts
wings and flies up
into the air,
a giant furry moth
that miaows.

'Never sleep with your tent open,'
she warns me, 'because
when The Flying Cat
finds its prey
it swoops down
and lands on it.

It sinks its claws
and its razor-sharp teeth
into its victim
and sucks its blood.
Slurp . . . Slurp . . . Slurp.'

We both shiver
and hold hands.
She doesn't like cats
and I don't like moths.

Just then something
blunders into the tent
flapping its wings.
'Miaow . . . miaow,' it says.
We hug each other.
We don't make a sound.
'Miaow . . . miaow . . .
slurp . . . slurp,' it says.

'Look, Simon,' we say,
'just go away, will you.
You aren't funny.'
We lie there quiet for a moment,
ignoring him.
At last I say, 'That's nothing.
Wait till you hear about
The Tree Creeper.

'It's like a huge brown
stick insect
which climbs
from tree to tree.
It hugs the branches,
waiting to drop down
on anyone
who walks underneath.

'Never pitch your tent
 under a tree,' I warn her,
'because if you do,
 in the middle of the night
The Tree Creeper
will drop down
and crawl inside
and crush you
in its stick-like arms.
Crunch! Crunch!'

Neither of us
likes that story.
I don't know where
I got such a horrid idea from.
We reach out
and hold hands.

Suddenly there is a
BANG!
as if half a tree
has landed
on top of the tent.

We scream
and hide our eyes.
We hear, 'Crunch, crunch, crunch.'
Then a silly laugh.

'Simon, you are stupid,' we say.
'You spoil everything.
Go away.'
Now my cousin
is very quiet.

I begin to think
perhaps I have won.
But then she says to me,
'You don't know about
The Invisible Man, do you?

'He can walk through walls
and see through doors.
He could pass through this tent
like a beam of light.
He could be standing there
by your side
and you wouldn't even see him.
You'd just feel him
breathing on you.

'It doesn't matter where
you pitch your tent,' she tells me.
'The Invisible Man
would get you.
Nothing could keep him out.'

Now it is really dark.
There isn't a sound.
I am lying here,
wide awake,
thinking about this monster
that is coming to get me
that I won't even
be able to see.

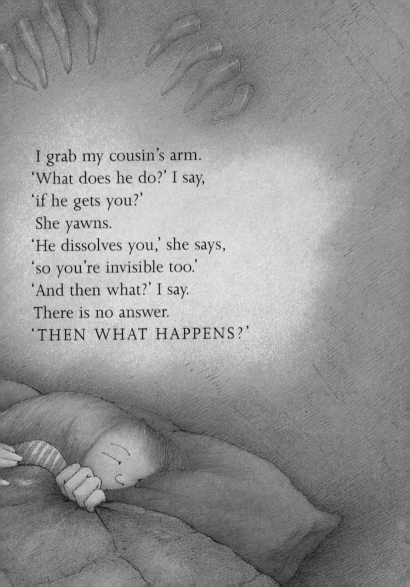

I grab my cousin's arm.
'What does he do?' I say,
'if he gets you?'
She yawns.
'He dissolves you,' she says,
'so you're invisible too.'
'And then what?' I say.
There is no answer.
'THEN WHAT HAPPENS?'

But my cousin has gone to sleep.
I can hear her
breathing through her mouth
as if she has
a peg on her nose.

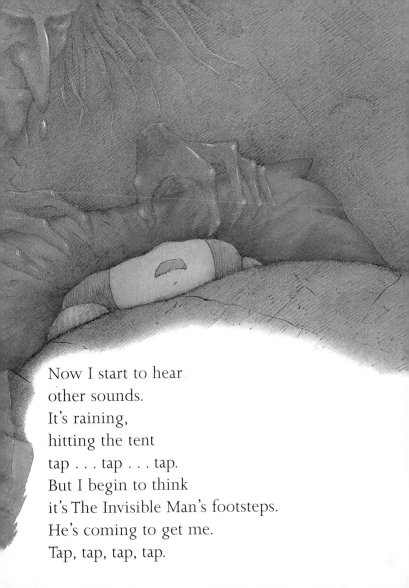

Now I start to hear
other sounds.
It's raining,
hitting the tent
tap . . . tap . . . tap.
But I begin to think
it's The Invisible Man's footsteps.
He's coming to get me.
Tap, tap, tap, tap.

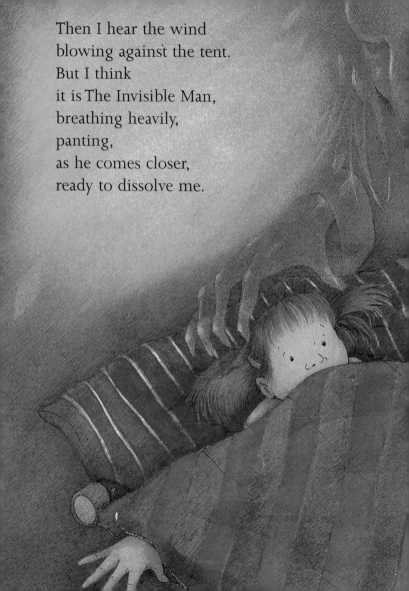

Then I hear the wind
blowing against the tent.
But I think
it is The Invisible Man,
breathing heavily,
panting,
as he comes closer,
ready to dissolve me.

I slide down
into my sleeping bag
and hide.

Now I can hear a ripping sound.
Someone is trying to get in.

I reach out for my torch
and switch it on
in time to see
the zip burst open
and a horrible face
appear in the gap.

'Can I come in?' says Simon.
'It's raining out here
and I'm getting wet.'
I take a deep breath.
'Oh Simon, you are stupid,' I say.
But I don't send him away.

He slides down
between me and my cousin
and we start to giggle.
Then I remember the picnic
we brought with us.
'Are you hungry?' I say.
Simon grins.

We sit up
in the torchlight,
side by side,
just the two of us,
eating our midnight feast.
We whisper
so we don't wake my cousin.
That would spoil everything.

In the morning
when she asks me
who ate her food
I shall tell her
it must have been
The Invisible Man.